RABID

RABID

Andalyn Powell

Bowtie Books

Copyright © 2026 by Andalyn Powell

All rights reserved.

No portion of this book may be reproduced in any form without written permission from the publisher or author, except as permitted by U.S. copyright law.

Paperback: 979-8-9941074-0-9

Ebook: 979-8-9941074-1-6

Library of Congress Control Number: 2026903111

Edited by Wendy Claunch and Dr. Andrea Leonard

To the misunderstood.
To those who feel alone in a crowded room.
To the Drakes of this world.

And to my best friend...
who holds my hand in the dark.

"Hold my hand…in…th-the dark."
      -Drake

CONTENTS

The Mood	1
1. Beige	3
2. Russet	13
3. Sepia	27
4. Umber	41
Epilogue	45
The World Undone	53
Acknowledgements	55
Author's Note	57
About the author	59
Leave A Review	61
Inside The Mind Of Rabid	63

THE MOOD

O*h! The bite, and the sting, and the pain which ensues,*
The insanity that percolates the mind straight through.
The fear of the water, which is safe to consume,
The foaming at the mouth and the dull brown room.
Should your symptoms show before medical assist,
You are slowly dying,
Your brain is liquifying,
And I would be lying,
If I didn't tell you this:
Rabies.
The futuristic variant is free,
If you value your existence, then you must flee.

One

BEIGE

The day was sunny and bright, but a strange unease hung in the air. There was no wind, just a sweltering heat and a subtle, buried panic that one could not necessarily place a finger on. Drake made his way steadily and straightforwardly down the road. He kept his hands in his pockets and his icy blue eyes focused ahead. He felt sad inside but made no expression. He continued to strut slowly, with a slightly aloof air. His face was thin, and the cheekbones were visible, giving him a cold and intelligent appearance. His stature was smaller than average, but he looked mildly strong. Although he projected a cold demeanor, his face was strangely handsome in a very youthful and delicate way. His dark wavy hair contrasted with his eyes, which further accented his cherry red lips and pale skin. No one would guess, from his appearance alone, that he was experiencing the hardest year of his life.

"No one to walk with me this afternoon," he thought. "Why? Why will no one walk with me?" His face tightened, and his mouth turned downward ever so slightly as these thoughts passed through his mind.

As he made his way along the road, his face returning to its expressionless default, he suddenly heard a dark and sinister growling, like that of a cat and dog together, yet very unlike those kinds of animals. It sounded much more savage and aggressive, unlike any sound that Drake had ever heard in his 22 years of existence. Drake ceased his calculated march and discovered a clearing in the trees on the side of the road. He turned his attention to the most prominent aspect of the clearing: a small, two-storied, abandoned building. At the side of the building was a small basketball net. On the dark pavement, underneath the basketball net, were a dog and a cat, growling and snarling in the heat, obviously the source of the unusual sound. Drake's expressionless face suddenly morphed to exhibit a barely noticeable note of surprise and intrigue. The animals appeared to be thirsty and heat-stricken. They both let slimy drool drip from their mouths, and their natural temperament seemed to be encased in a profound instinct to survive.

Drake combed his fingers through his hair, nervously, and stepped toward them, cautiously. He felt a twinge of deep empathy for the creatures, even though his face did not show it. His glaring blue eyes focused coldly on the objects of the strange noise. Not only was Drake surprisingly empathetic, but he was also curious and quite willing to share the additional water that he carried inside his backpack. He halted for a brief moment to unzip his backpack and retrieve the water container and a small bowl. He poured the water into the bowl, rezipped the backpack, and vigilantly made his way forward, as the animals snarled at him.

"These animals must be extremely thirsty," he thought, as he observed the animals' savage appearances. His mouth continued to display no curve indicative of either uplifting or depressed emotion. He merely made his way forward in the same aloof and quiet manner in which he had previously strutted down the road. All of a sudden, Drake felt a rush of courage and began to quicken his advances. His face remained expressionless, but his muscles tensed determinedly. The animals began to bark and hiss furiously, as Drake thrust the bowl in front of them.

"There!" said Drake assertively. "I have brought you a drink!" His cold blue eyes flashed.

Just as Drake concluded his bold action, the dog rushed at him, leaving no time for Drake to bolt away, and bit him vigorously on the wrist. Drake pulled his wrist away instinctively and recoiled in extreme discomfort. His blank countenance suddenly came alive: his face clenched in pain and his piercing blue eyes flashed even more fiercely. The bite seemed to press into his skin as a thousand needles. It was more painful than the sting of the most aggressive hornet, and it caused Drake to shout, "All I wanted was to give you some water!" Even animals didn't want to be friends with him, it seemed. Pain. Pain. This pain was unlike any he had ever experienced in his life. He looked down at his wrist. It was bleeding profusely. It throbbed. His head spun. He felt like he was dying, and he collapsed to the ground.

The dog suddenly ceased growling. It began to whimper and sauntered humbly towards Drake and began to lick the injured wrist. The pain was beginning to subside. Drake's face softened, and one side of his mouth turned faintly upward. "That's alright," he replied, as he slowly got up, still cringing with lingering twinges of pain. However, the emotional pain of loneliness felt less, if only for a second. The dog liked him now...even just a little bit. He felt the urge to remain close to these strange animals and even play with them.

He was lonely.

Desperate for connection, Drake, setting aside the bowl of water, which remained untouched by the animals, unzipped his backpack a second time to reveal a basketball. The dog leaped into the air, yapping, as Drake, pushing past the extreme pain of his wound, hurled the basketball into the netted hoop attached to the side of the building. The cat purred and rubbed its face against Drake's leg. The dog nudged the ball toward Drake. Drake fixed his piercing gaze on the dog for a moment, then reached for the ball and hurled it through the hoop again. This cautious enjoyment prevailed for quite some time. Drake became more and more relaxed as he played with the unknown animals. He made two new friends today. That was more than he had made in the past year.

Suddenly, Drake's face twitched momentarily, and his cold stare met with that of the hot ball of fire in the heavens. The sun was now located half the distance between the sky's zenith and the horizon. He glanced down at his wrist again. It had stopped bleeding, but there was now an ugly brownish wound upon the skin. His eyes widened slightly as he saw it. Drake, deciding he should begin the trek home, unzipped his backpack and placed the basketball within. He patted the dog on the head, stroked the cat, and said aloud, "I will be back tomorrow." He was exhausted from his long day of adventures and was quite ready to return home to prepare himself a hot meal and a dressing for his wound. He turned matter-of-factly toward the road.

Drake was not entirely prepared for what met his gaze when he turned around. In fact, the sight that he beheld made him break his reserved demeanor altogether and gasp in utter terror and fright. The road, which he had naturally been expecting to catch sight of, was about a hundred feet below him. He was no longer standing on a level boundary between the building and the road, he was standing on a ledge, which, if he lost his balance, could hurtle him to a brutal or even fatal injury.

All of a sudden, Drake began to feel hot and dizzy. Intuitively, he hurled himself to the ground, which was now above ground, on top of, and away from, the ledge. He realized that if he did not escape the ledge within the next second, the dizziness would cause him to plummet. Terror filled his soul, and his eyes bulged. His mouth felt dry, and he felt an unreal horror. How could any of this be real? This was not understandable nor realistic by any means. Fog clouded his brain and left him unable to reason. After a few seconds, Drake mustered the strength to leap to his feet and began making his way around the front porch of the building. The porch was surrounded by a wooden rail, which would protect him from another encounter of bare horror.

Drake trekked the length of the porch and, discovering no logical method of escape, finally tried the front door. It was unlocked and creaked slightly as it opened. Drake's heart was racing, and a foreign anxiety, almost a panic, set in as he gazed upon the dreariness of the abandoned building's interior. Its entire aura was that of a dull brown nightmare. The brown of the room was very similar to the color of his wound, he thought. Cobwebs existed in abundance, and the floor consisted of ancient wooden boards, which squeaked like evil rats. The windows of the front wall, which contained the door, were stained glass, and the light of a beginning sunset shone through them, illuminating and amplifying the dreariness and loneliness of the dull brown atmosphere within. The contrast of the stained glass with the brown back wall and floors created a sense of absolute and unexplained trepidation. Drake breathed deeply, but the odor was foreign, like nothing he had ever smelled before. It was rotten, but he was unable to identify it. Along the back wall was a battered couch of an extremely muted crimson color, badly in need of upholstering. It appeared to be solidified with age and painfully hard.

Drake stumbled through the door and entered fully into the building. His mouth twitched as he glanced to the side, and he noticed a sturdy wooden antique table. Upon the table was a tablecloth, matching the same muted crimson color of the couch. Upon the tablecloth was a loaf of bread and a chunk of orange cheese. Drake felt himself drawn to the bread and cheese in an almost unnatural way. It was as if the food had placed him in a trance and was able to control his mind and actions. Drake began to desperately crave the contents on the tablecloth and felt that he was beginning to lose his sense of rationality and collected resolve. He lurched forward, rapidly consuming a large portion of the bread and cheese. As he ate, he growled and grunted like an animal. It tasted awful. It was moldy and stale, yet Drake continued to feel a magnetic pull toward the food, as if he must have more and more of it. As he gorged himself, grunting, snarling, and drooling, he experienced a panicked feeling of guilt and loss of control. It was as though his identity was being invaded by another version of himself. Drake wondered if he was losing his sanity. His sanity was the only thing that made him feel human at this point in his life, and now that would be gone, too. It was terrifying, but nonetheless, he continued in his reckless actions, feeling that hope was beyond him, and that the only thing that could possibly save him was his survival instinct.

When Drake had consumed every morsel, he staggered to the couch and fell upon it. The guilt and dismay at his animalistic behavior weighed him down so heavily that he felt he could do nothing else but lie upon the couch and attempt a rest. As he lay upon the couch, he thought of home, the lonely home he would go to if he were able to leave. He would open his lonely door, crawl up the lonely stairs to his lonely room, crawl into his lonely bed, and sleep a lonely sleep. If only he had some friends. If only he had some people to invite into his lonely home. But no one would talk to him. Why? Why would no one talk to him? He felt so alone right now. Even his lonely home seemed better than the hard crimson couch in the dull brown room.

There was a room in his house where he would go to imagine away his loneliness. It was a dark room, cool (he hated heat), and very quiet. Drake would go in there, shut the door, drink in the cool air, and imagine that he had circles of friends and caring people surrounding him, telling him how much they loved him. Sometimes, he imagined just one very special friend, in the dark with him, not saying anything, holding his hand, and making him not feel lonely. She would be enough. As he thought these thoughts, Drake's eyes became heavier. The world became darker in color as he embraced sleep, the one thing that could allow him escape from this horror, if only for a moment.

Drake felt his consciousness flicker as he knocked at the door of sleep. His oddly simultaneous desire to return to complete consciousness was countered by an inability to wake. His brain tingled in readiness to fall through an open door, but a fast and unmoved partition barred him from mindless relief. Drake could only taste the outer edge of complete and peaceful unconsciousness. Yet, for a reason he did not understand, he was unable to fully return to the light of consciousness. Light and dark merged into brown, and reality seemed to be tainted and unreachable. He felt that he was trapped within a tiny space between two obstructing partitions.

The only awareness Drake possessed during this episode was that of a dull brown color, just the color of the impression which had haunted him as he had entered this battered room. It was as though he could see the room through his eyelids while he half-slept, and he felt the sheer horror of being left alone within a half-conscious, dull brown nightmare. It was a color of confusion and muddled reasoning. For a few awful moments, during this state, and for the first time in his life, his mind felt almost completely dead. He had no thoughts. He was mindless. His only consciousness was a rushing noise in his ears and the sense of still being alive. Sometimes he felt the hardness of the couch. But that was it. There were only feelings. Lonely. So lonely. Nobody to talk to. His mind could not retain any information necessary to sleep or wake. He could do nothing. His mind was brown. It was dull brown. Paralysis. He dipped in and out of thoughtlessness and thoughts over and over and over. What was happening to him? Was this house a place of insanity, where those who entered lost their true identity and faculty of logical reasoning? He must get out. He must get out. He must get out...before it is too late. He must wake up, or fall asleep, or something else...what was it? Paralysis. Dull brown. His mind was brown. He could not remember. The hardness of the couch. Brown. Dull brown. What was he doing? Was he alive or dead? What was reality and life? Did it really exist? Was he losing all of this? Was he losing his mind? Why would nobody talk to him? Lonely. So lonely. Wake up! He could not. Paralysis. Nothing but dull brown and thoughts belonging to the insane.

After many hours spent shrouded in this unknown state, Drake suddenly felt a rush of adrenaline. It was a feeling that he had never experienced before. It was unlike an ordinary adrenaline rush. It was much more potent, and Drake felt it throughout his entire being. It was as if his entire body had been injected with pure strength. He felt as though he suddenly broke through the partition between the middle world and waking consciousness with his fist, and he jolted awake, violently. Sweat poured from his hair as he instinctively realized that he had escaped the insane nightmare world of irrationality and lost cognition. Dreams had always been a source of inspiration and mental activity for him, but this nightmare had made him realize that the opposite was now possible, and he never wanted to do it again. He lay there unmoving, with his characteristic expressionlessness, for some time as he gradually adjusted to his newly awakened state.

Two
RUSSET

When Drake gained full consciousness, his first sensation was extreme thirst. The dizziness had become more dominant, and Drake felt that he would suffocate if he did not breathe in fresh, cool air to alleviate the feverish heat. He attempted to sit up. This drained him, and he sat on the couch for a full ten minutes without movement. As he sat, he noticed that a glass of water had been placed upon the table that had held the previously consumed store of food. He also noticed a lamp, located on the far right side of the room, which shut out the darkness of the now present night with its illumination. Someone must have turned on the lamp and placed the glass of water on the table as he was in his unconventional state of consciousness. Drake realized that he was not alone in the building, and he felt a pin prick of hope pierce his anxious mind. If someone else were also trapped here, the nightmare might not be as terrible as it now was. He glanced at the area on his wrist where the dog had bitten him. It was still there. An ugly brown wound. It was tingling. He shook it, as though that would make it stop tingling.

At last, his thirst became so unbearable that Drake resolved to stand up and reach for the glass of transparent liquid. Determined to quench his thirst, Drake staggered toward the table and grasped the glass. He held it to his lips, but hesitated. His mouth twitched. Something inside him, something so subtle that it was almost undetectable, made him feel uneasy. It was as though something within his mind was warning him not to drink the water. It seemed so irrational and trivial that Drake pushed aside the feeling and took a gigantic swig of water. It felt cool, and it gushed slowly across his tongue. As he swallowed, he felt a foreign tightness within his throat. Drake began to choke and gag violently. He felt as though death were coming for him, as he gasped for air. He ran to the couch and fell upon it, still choking. He clawed at the rough crimson fabric of the couch as he gagged and writhed. Finally, a few meager drops of the water finally claimed victory over the guards of his throat, and his wrestle with death ended in a gulp of air. Drake, now feeling hydrated, but shaken, resolved to rest for a minute before he attempted to find the strange one who had placed the water on the table.

As Drake lay on the couch, he caught a glimpse of something which he had not noticed in his state of extreme dehydration and feverishness. A door, facing toward the left end of the couch, stood closed, but contained a tiny window which revealed a small deck attached to the side of the building. Drake got up, walked toward the door, and tried the knob. The door opened, and Drake felt a cool night wind lick the side of his face. He closed his eyes and gradually inhaled the fresh air that he had longed for inside the musty and stifling atmosphere of the building. It had been hot in there. He hated heat. As he inhaled, he felt even less dehydrated and feverish. It was as if air could somehow be a substitute for water and quench his thirst. Cool air. Glorious cool air. He made his way to the rail of the deck and peered down over the edge. He was still too far above the ground for an attempt at escape, but at least he felt free in the wind and cool air for a moment.

As he stood on the deck, Drake's thoughts began to wander. He thought about his town, and how crowded and noisy and full of unimportant people it was. He thought about his home and wondered if he had locked the door before he left. He thought about his favorite room and how much the night wind reminded him of the feeling he got when he was inside. He thought about the imaginary friends who surrounded and loved him when he was inside – and the one special friend who said nothing but held his hand in the darkness. However, no matter how many places Drake's mind explored, nor how many dimensions crossed his cognitive capabilities, one single, subtle image and concept, which disturbed him for a reason he could not quite grasp, seemed to stay burned in his subconscious: the transparent liquid, water. His wrist was tingling. He scratched it. He tried to continue thinking about home, and his room, and how to escape the strange building, but his thoughts constantly turned to focus on the image, and he found himself imagining oceans and rivers flooding the earth and choking him out of the very universe. In his mind, waterfalls gushed over him, and he broke out with a strange disease. Drake scratched his wrist even harder. Ponds and pools overflowed and chased him forever. Most terrifying of all, what his mind feared most was the image of a simple glass of water. He wanted to reach out and take the glass, to drink its contents freely, but he seemed to be paralyzed, and this paralysis brought him to a rush of terror. He was parched but was unable to satisfy one of his most basic and vital needs, and he could not understand why. Drake was scratching his wrist so aggressively now that it was bleeding. Even now, he could not think about his favorite room without imagining it flooded with hot black water. He was drowning, and no one was holding his hand in the darkness. Drake stopped scratching his wrist. Tears of fear and grief rolled down his cheeks as he stared, his face unmoved, at the stars in the night sky. He was scared and alone.

After a full thirty minutes of enduring the torture of the wanderings of his mind, Drake abruptly, but halfheartedly, sniffled, wiped the bloody brown wound on his shirt, turned toward the door, opened it, and entered back into the building. The refreshment of the night wind had been ruined by his thoughts. When Drake entered, he was startled and astonished by the sight which he beheld. Numerous people were congregated inside, jabbering in a low rumble amongst themselves, and enjoying platters of bread and cheese that were being passed around generously. Drake pinned his body against the wall, not wanting to move for fear that the crowd would notice him. He had the strange feeling that he should not be here. Drake noticed that the bread and cheese were just as moldy as that which he had found upon the table earlier, nonetheless the strange-looking people appeared not to notice. They seemed to enjoy it, oblivious to the unhealthy aspect, which surely would frighten them beyond reason if they were to notice it. Drake wondered why they were unable to notice how moldy and disgusting the food appeared. Suddenly, his own irrational craving for it became extremely potent, but this time, he was somehow able to ignore his feelings in an effort to appear polite (perhaps because of the partial rejuvenation of the night wind, earlier).

Drake hated people. Well, he hated strangers. They were the ones who made him sad. The ones who didn't care. The ones who made him feel lonely. Drake brushed aside his sad thoughts and gazed around the room once more, observing the scene. He stepped in a little farther. They were dressed in odd white robes stained with brown flecks and spots. The spots and flecks were the same brown color, which Drake imagined when he thought of the room as a brown nightmare. He shuddered as he remembered the nothing world where he had been trapped as he had attempted sleep. He thought he might never be able to sleep again for fear of becoming trapped a second time. However potently terrifying this thought was to him, Drake pushed it aside and continued to observe the strange people. They varied in appearance but seemed to have the same voice: a low, systematic rumbling and fear-inducing timbre. The terms and voice-type they used sounded familiar, but Drake could not quite place where he had heard these voices or words before. They each carried a strange instrument with them. Not a musical instrument, but a...what was it? Each was different, anyhow. Every now and then, tiny clusters of bubbles seemed to float from their mouths as they socialized. It was random and sporadic, but Drake noticed that it happened often. They shuffled about the room randomly, moving from corner to corner and shifting position quite frequently. To Drake, it also seemed that the people shifted shape, but there were so many of them that he was not quite sure if this was truth or illusion conceived by his own mind. The strange people held glasses of water, like the one Drake had found on the table, and induced an atmosphere that might have been considered pleasant to some. Drake cringed as he saw the water glasses and felt the urge to run, but he stayed out of curiosity. The strange people were not close enough to do him any harm with the water, he told himself. They did not even seem to see him, even though some looked right at him. As Drake observed more closely, he also noticed that, though the people held glasses of water, not a single person took a sip.

Drake noticed, in the middle of the crowd, standing still, a tall, middle-aged man. He was dressed in a sterile white robe and wore a strange white bathing cap. He also wore a pair of white gloves, which gave a touch of elegance to his attire. He also carried an instrument, but his was bigger and appeared more powerful than the rest. His beard was short, neat, and gray, and his nose was rather large but thin. When Drake saw his eyes, he noticed them immediately. They were an unearthly grey color and seemed to cut into his very mind. Drake stepped shyly forward. His mouth twitched.

The man approached him and said, "Welcome to our gathering. Please make yourself comfortable. My name is Noitanicullah, but you may refer to me as Noitan."

Drake touched his ears in surprise. Noitan's voice sounded strange, hollow, almost as though it were echoing inside his own head.

Drake replied timidly, but firmly, "I am Drake."

The man nodded his head in affirmation. Drake shuffled his feet awkwardly. He was not used to people talking to him.

"Who are these others?" he questioned Noitan, in a monotone voice, which indicated that the question required a brief, straightforward, and to-the-point answer.

"They are the Enigami. They provide me with company. They are beings like myself, but I am slightly different. We live here quite happily and simply. We enjoy our unembellished meals of bread, cheese, and wa-wa-wa-ter, and we enjoy each other's presence each evening for dinner."

Drake noticed the strange and trembling tone of Noitan's voice as he pronounced the word "water."

As this conversation continued, Drake noticed that the same clusters of bubbles floated from Noitan's mouth as from the mouths of the Enigami.

Drake's cold stare panned the room, once again, before he began, hesitantly, "How may I leave?" He had finally asked the question that he had been desperately craving an answer to ever since he had become imprisoned in this horrible place.

Noitan seemed not to hear the question. "There are many things that we do here," he said. The Enigami's voice rose and fell rumblingly in rhythm around them.

Drake, surprised, and beginning to feel an instinctual twinge of anxiety, tried again. "May I leave this building?"

Noitan once again seemed completely oblivious to the question and continued, "We make the bread and cheese each morning and the rest..." Noitan's voice became a whisper, "...the rest is stored in a secret room upstairs."

Drake began to feel very uneasy. The Enigami's one voice became louder and more rumbling. It dipped up and down uncomfortably.

"Is there any way out of this building?" he asked a third time. "I want to go home."

Noitan's face remained the same as he said, "We would be very happy if you would join us, Drake."

Drake's mouth twitched multiple times. The Enigami's voice was now inside his head, just like Noitan's. What if they stole his mind? What if his mind became brown again?

Finally losing his patience and beginning to feel a severe panic rising within his chest, he suddenly broke his reserve and shouted at the top of his lungs, "Do you not hear me!? I want to go home!" Drake snarled and growled, uncharacteristically.

He was not surprised when Noitan, nor the people around him, seemed not to even sense his cries of frustration, nor his animalistic utterances. Noitan, appearing nonchalant, put his hand on

Drake's shoulder in a friendly manner. The touch was like icy electricity. Drake suddenly began to feel feverish again.

"I would enjoy a rest, actually," said Drake in a monotone voice, unsure of how else to reply. Drake looked down at his shirt and noticed that the same tiny bubbles that erupted from the mouths of Noitan and the Enigami were erupting from him, too. They were cascading from his mouth and onto his shirt in torrents. The icy electricity from Noitan's hand resting on his shoulder continued to rush through his veins and made him feel sick. Noitan nodded his head in the same manner he had when Drake had introduced himself, removed his hand from Drake's shoulder, and turned to mingle with the crowd once again.

Drake stumbled toward the couch and flopped onto it weakly. He rubbed his shirt against the couch to remove the bubbles. They were not coming out of his mouth anymore. He groaned as the feverishness intensified. His glazed eyes focused on the unwanted crowd congregated near his resting place. He began to feel helplessly annoyed by the Enigami, especially with their glasses of water. He scowled at them with a cold stare and wished that they would disappear and leave him to suffer alone. He wanted to be alone. He did not need anyone. He did not want anyone to hold his hand in the dark. He just wanted them all to go away. He scratched his wrist. As Drake watched the Enigami, feeling very irritated, he suddenly began, once again, to feel the same strange warning in his mind that he had felt when he had first held the glass to his lips. The memory of his choking fit and the intuitive sense of caution returned to his mind. This time the warning was much stronger and began to creep over him and intensify into a violent fear. Drake continued to watch the Enigami intently, and his cold stare evolved into a hot, mad glare. He curled his arms and legs into his body and pressed himself closely to the couch as they passed him. He felt dizzy, hot, and anxious. If any of the water spilled from the Enigami's glasses, it might spill on him. Drake held his protective position on the couch and continued to gape ahead with a glazed, mad stare. He looked down at his shirt. The bubbles were cascading onto it again. He brushed his shirt against the couch, but the second they were gone, more appeared to replace them. He repeated this cycle a few times. They were wet bubbles. They were wet and angry. They were white, but he thought of them as brown. He glanced up. The water glasses were coming closer. He knew he must immediately escape the Enigami, but he was too terrified to move. All at once, the Enigami next to the couch made their way toward the antique table, and Drake saw his chance. He leapt off the couch and rushed to the right side of the room, dripping bubbles on the floor as he ran, and finally hid behind and under a wooden desk that supported the lamp.

As Drake concealed himself under the desk, he heard the voices of the Enigami chattering and guffawing. He shuddered as he realized that he could also hear the clinking of the water glasses against each other. Ouch. His wrist was throbbing. He clutched the side of the desk. It was rough and contained many splinters. He brushed his wound thoughtlessly against it. Drake prayed that none of the Enigami would find him here. He knew that if they finally noticed him, they might force him to drink. They would cover him in water. They would drown him. These thoughts made him feel faint. His fever worsened, and he lay on the ground, attempting to sleep and trying to convince himself that he was safe under the desk, but sleep avoided him as the gazelle avoids the lion.

Drake noticed a door a few feet to his left. It was a beautiful door. It was wooden, as were the other doors, but this door was ornate and ancient. It was purple and gold, and it seemed to glow. It did not fit the mood of the building at all. It seemed to Drake a haven from his misery. Perhaps, behind it, there was a room like his room at home. He slowly got to his feet and staggered toward the door. He let out his breath slowly, his mind primed for vital relief, as he put his hand to the knob. All at once, he heard the voice of Noitan.

"STOP!"

Drake turned around abruptly and found Noitan towering fiercely above him. The Enigami had ceased their babbling and banqueting. They were now turned toward Noitan and Drake with dark, expressionless countenances. It seemed to Drake that they were now rumbling very quietly, but in a different tone. It was as if they were chanting, "Stop. Stop. Stop." repeatedly in that one voice. The brown spots and flecks on their white robes stood out more strongly than ever.

Noitan continued to speak, and his voice became low and serious. "You will not go in there, nor will you ask questions concerning this door."

With that, he retrieved an elaborate-looking key from his pocket, shuffled Drake out of the way, and locked the door. He calmly returned to the Enigami and continued his social feasting. The Enigami resumed their synchronous babbling and acted as if nothing had occurred to tear them away from the present. Drake's heart sank, and his anxiety returned stronger than ever. He returned to his desk hideaway with a zombie-like sluggishness. The bubbles had stopped, but he was shaky and hot inside. He hated heat.

It felt as though he hid under the desk for hours. His tortured mind hurtled from one thought to another as he listened to the strange tone of the Enigami's seemingly single voice. During the points when the one voice, consisting of many voices, became louder, excited, and more energetic, Drake's panic heightened, and his muscles tightened in readiness to fight or flee should the Enigami approach him with the dreaded water. When the voice of the Enigami fluctuated to a quieter, calmer, and barely audible rumble, Drake's mind and muscles relaxed for a short time, preparing to begin the cycle once again when the voice next triggered his senses.

Drake truly believed that the night would last for eternity. The water glasses became a nightmarish rumination, and his throat tightened so that he choked. His throat! He could not breathe. His throat was tight. His throat was brown. Dull brown. He rubbed his wrist against the splintery desk even harder. His wound was now dripping blood onto the floor. The perpetual rhythm of tightening and relaxing his muscles became second nature to him as he looked into the reverberating chambers of eternity, only to find no end. His mind sought a boundary, but eternity continued, as a chamber which looped back into itself. Drake felt, in his mind, that he was darting through the looping chamber over and over again, driving himself mad at the thought of never getting out, of never returning to reality and security.

Just as Drake wobbled dangerously on the border between sanity and pure insanity, the voice of the Enigami ceased altogether. Drake's muscles tightened instinctively, and his alarm heightened to its zenith. He dug his palms into the most splintery part of the desk. Blood was gushing mercilessly from his wound and starting to drip from new splinter wounds on his hands. He waited for the Enigami to come find him. He knew they would come, clutching the thing that caused his borderline insanity: the glasses of transparent liquid. He backed further into the darkness under the desk and listened, muscles burning with tension. He heard nothing. At last, he heard the sound of a key in a lock and the opening of a door. From the location of the sound, Drake guessed that the door being opened was the one that he had been forbidden to enter. The sound of footsteps on stairs caught Drake's perked ears. Drake felt a twinge of hope. He was to be free at last from the intruding presence of the Enigami. He would be alone. He didn't need anyone to hold his hand in the dark.

As soon as Drake heard the door close, he bolted from under the desk and scanned the room for water glasses. No glasses were to be found. Drake suddenly felt a peace that he thought he could never encounter again. The eternal nightmare, which he had experienced under the desk, was over, and he felt exhausted. His eyes turned in the direction of the door, and he shuffled curiously toward it, cautiously trying the handle. It was locked. Noitan must have locked the door behind himself and the Enigami. Drake wondered what was behind the door and why it was forbidden for him to enter, but he was currently too fatigued to allow these questions to prey upon his mind. He still felt extremely feverish and dizzy. He quietly returned to the desk to switch off the small lamp that lit the room's interior. He then stumbled toward the couch and lay down upon it. He fell asleep immediately.

Three

SEPIA

Drake was startled awake by the massive drumming of thunder. The lightning flashes seemed to fry the universe and were visible through the tiny window in the door, which led to the small deck. These phenomena brought Drake to a fully conscious state, and he sat up violently, sweat pouring from his skin. His fever had worsened, and his parched tongue felt heavy and cumbersome. His wrist was so painful that he could barely move it without unbearable pain shooting through his entire body. He looked down at it. It was very dark brown now and looked larger than before. He scratched it, then howled at the pain it caused. As he listened to the sounds of the storm, the dizziness he felt was overwhelming, and a searing and startling terror was felt within his being. It was not the nimble lightning, nor the dominant thunder, which he feared, but another sound. The horror it induced shook his internal sanity to its very core. The sound was cascading droplets, coming together as an army, demanding entry into the building.

From the moment Drake had noticed the sound of the water, the showers pouring to the earth dynamically, his sanity snapped, and he lost control of his mind and senses. The entire room shifted and became smaller. Drake heard sounds that did not exist, but nonetheless, drove him mad. Whenever the lightning flashed, Drake imagined holes in the walls of the tiny building, with the water gushing in through them. The water was no longer a clear and transparent liquid, but seemed to be colored black. Drake had never seen a black so dark before. It was a black so unearthly that it didn't seem to exist. The very color of the liquid signaled death to him, and it foamed viciously as it entered the building. Whenever a new hole appeared, Drake heard a rushing noise that seemed to exist only in his ears. This was coupled with a few brief seconds of paralysis each time. At the end of each paralysis, Drake's mouth filled with liquid, and he tasted what he thought was the black liquid. These moments filled him with a deadly panic: the foamy bubbles were back, more of them than before. He spewed them from his mouth in an attempt to purge himself of the liquid. The bubbles were wet and brown, and they were choking him. His wrist hurt so much now that he wished he could remove it from his body. As he looked down at the bite wound, he noticed that it had transformed into a black hole. It was the same deathly black of the water, and Drake had the urge to scoop up some of the liquid on the floor and pour it into the black hole on his wrist. Of course, he could not do this because of his intense fear of the water. No matter how much he wanted to, he could not, and this made him feel crazy.

Drake dashed madly from one corner of the room to another, choking and gagging, with nowhere to escape, scratching his wrist aggressively, as more and more holes appeared in the walls. He shouted and screamed until his voice was hoarse, foam continuing to pour from his mouth. His entire body was drenched in sweat, and his heart beat in his chest, as if it were pounding on a door and demanding to be released from the sheer panic. He leapt in the air several times to avoid his feet touching the water. He shrieked and twisted his arms in the manner of a lunatic. His very soul was shaken, and the terror he felt was indescribable. In his mind, the thing he feared most was now attacking him in a more horrible form, and there was nowhere for him to hide. The water would now have him and would make him choke again, until he was unable to breathe. Suffocation would be his fate. His mind continued to trick him with hallucinations and strange sensory illusions. Finally, Drake, realizing that the water was about to fully cover the floor, danced between the liquid rivers running beside his feet and avoided them with intuitive precision, rushed to the couch, perched upon its topmost backing, and huddled against the wall. He growled and hissed at the water. Foam spattered from his mouth, and he beat the wall in anger. He brushed the couch to remove the bubbles, but they kept coming back. His wrist throbbed. He scratched it.

Drake uttered incomprehensible sounds, and words poured forth that tried to communicate something, but were mixed up. Drake sat perched on the couch for hours, his mind weirdly morphing and changing the water and the layout of the room. The room became his special room at home. It was flooded. There was nowhere for him to go now. His room was brown. Dull brown. The laws of physics seemed to be disturbed and utterly ignored altogether. One second, he was upon the couch, the next, the desk. Finally, his mind bent into colors and shapes, where black, brown, and a mysterious, shifting shape were the only things it detected. There was no taste, sound, tactile feeling, or smell. This form of consciousness was dominated only by a dull brown background and the black shifting shape. Drake's sanity was gone, but even in his lunacy, he knew the shape was the water, which he dreaded. He saw it surround him and come closer and closer. Drake felt himself falling into the shape, and he lost consciousness.

When Drake awoke, he could sense the room again, instead of just shapes and colors; however, his sanity was not fully restored. The storm had ended in the night, and it was morning. Drake's ears rang, and his head felt pressurized. He discovered that he could barely sit up due to the dizziness. His fever was still extremely high, but lower than last night, and his mouth was so parched that he could barely open it without gagging. Although he felt dehydrated beyond belief, he knew that he could not ingest that evil black liquid. It would surely kill him before he died of thirst. The strange foamy bubbles were gushing from his mouth in great amounts. It was everywhere, and he had to wipe his mouth multiple times with his shirt. The pain in his wrist was excruciating, and he held up his arm to check it again. He gasped weakly. It was even uglier than before. It was as though it had widened and spread up to part of his hand. He could not look at it without feeling sick to his stomach. It was a large, gaping, ugly brown hole that festered and glared at him. He scratched it, but immediately realized that this still caused the horrible pangs in his body. He felt them in his very brain. He lay still and stared directly in front of him. The door to the deck seemed to glower back at him fiercely. Its brown color seemed so vivid that it appeared unreal, and its matter seemed to crawl and oscillate strangely and pulsate with the beat of his heart. He wanted to fall asleep again to escape the miserable feeling of weakness, but he knew that he would wake up feeling even worse if he was able to successfully drift off into unconsciousness. The very air seemed to smother him, and his parched tongue was a burden pressing heavily upon his waking self. It was very hot. He hated heat.

    Drake moaned in miserable distress. He wished, even in his state of semi-sanity, to go home and have all of this be a nightmare. He didn't care if he was alone. He just wanted to go home to his room, his cool air, and his imaginary world of friends. Noitan and the Enigami were strange beings. Perhaps they were the ones who had cast a spell on this awful place. They had to be the reason Drake was unable to leave. They certainly possessed strange ways, and the fact that the door to the upstairs was open to all but him was most definitely suspicious. So, although, at this moment, Drake had limited reasoning capabilities, he tossed these ideas around within the chambers of his mind and lay helpless on the couch, dreading the moment when Noitan would unlock the door to the upstairs, Enigami following him. He knew that he would be unable to defend himself against the Enigami in his current state.

They would surely bring the water glasses with them, mutter in their singular low voice, and when they found him, they would force him to drink. Anxiety rose in his chest, but he was too exhausted to let it overtake him. At last, the moment Drake had been dreading occurred, and the key to the upstairs door was turned in the lock, and the door was opened. Noitan stepped into the room.

When Drake craned his neck around, from where he lay, to catch a glimpse of Noitan, his heart began to beat double time. Noitan was barely recognizable, except for his intense grey eyes, which now contained bright red circles, like targets, around them as they glared fiercely at Drake. His face was snow white and appeared powdery, as the face of the eldest of the old. His white cap was gone, and his hair looked as though he had been trying to tear it out. Blood dripped onto his forehead. His face also appeared disfigured, as though he were very sick. He coughed and spewed bubbles from his mouth so fast that Drake was afraid the room would flood as it did last night. He seemed to be enveloped in a giant brown cloak, which shifted form so often that it was hard to look at with the naked eye. Drake tried to observe exactly when the cloak shifted form, each time, but no matter how hard his mind operated, he was unable to notice the shift. He pounded his head in frustrated agony, but, although he could tell that something had changed, he could not understand how it had changed.

Noitan's new appearance did not frighten him half as much as the object Noitan held out to Drake. It was a water glass, but the liquid inside was not transparent, as it should be. Instead, it appeared to be identical to the terrifying liquid that Drake had seen last night, during the storm. It was the same deadly deep black color and seemed unreal compared to the very real glass.

Noitan continued to hold the glass out to Drake and repeat the word, "Drink."

Noitan's voice was different. It seemed deeper, louder, and more alien than before.

Bubbles gushed from his mouth as he cried, "Drink!" Noitan continued to repeat. "Drink. Drink. Drink the wa-wa-wa-ter."

Each time Noitan spoke, the ringing in Drake's ears fluctuated with his voice tone and volume, as if Noitan were a part of the auditory region of Drake's brain. Drake covered his ears and continued to wipe his mouth on his shirt. The room spun and he felt himself going into a panic. He must act now, or he will be forced to drink and die.

Drake got up from the couch, slowly, the room still spinning. He could not move any faster or he might slip. He was shaking violently, and his mind was racing. He navigated his way to the door, which led to the small deck, with only intuition as his guide. At last, he put his hand to the knob, opened the door with a frantic gesture, and stumbled out wildly onto the deck. The sky was bright, but the day was just as hot as it had been the day before, and Drake felt that the heat added to the immense feeling of fever. He hated heat. He scratched his wrist. Brown pain shot through his body. His heart raced as he watched Noitan follow him out onto the deck. He screamed in terror. He was cornered, and there was no escape. He wanted to be lonely! He did not need someone to hold his hand in the dark! He tore at his wrist. More brown pain.

His panic reached its climax as Noitan came ever closer with the water. He began to pull his hair crazily as he realized that he would have to touch the water and possibly swallow it - no! He could not even think about it without feeling his insanity deepening. He banged his wrist against the rail of the deck. Brown, brown, brown pain! Blood spritzed onto the wood as his wound opened up again.

Suddenly, with tunnel vision, Drake noticed that the Enigami were following Noitan in his march across the porch. They did not appear as they had last night but seemed only to be impressions of faces within a massive crowd. Their faces were just as disfigured and sickly as Noitan's face, and the bubbles were pouring from their mouths. The faces merged together and shifted as strangely as Noitan's robe. The faces appeared as one single brown cloak, with multiple sickly pallid and wrinkled hands protruding from it. This cloak also shifted and was just as perplexing as the cloak which shrouded Noitan. Drake's mind became paralyzed as it tried to understand the cloak's unknowable form. Drake yelped in crazy terror and tugged out handfuls of hair as he realized that the Enigami also held glasses of the dark liquid.

They followed Noitan in the zombie-like repetition of the phrase, "Drink". Their collective voices caused the ringing in Drake's ears to intensify each time they spoke the word.

"Drink. Drink. Drink."

The ringing became unbearably ominous. He screamed and jumped up and down on the porch in a fit of near lunacy. There was absolutely no hope now.

As Drake jumped up and down crazily, he had the sense to notice that the Enigami were also carrying something else: platters of the same moldy bread and cheese which Drake had so heavily craved when he had first arrived. Now that Drake was seeing the food again, the craving was so strong that he lurched his body forward an inch, then stepped back, repeatedly. The foamy liquid gushed from his mouth once again, as he stared hungrily at the spoiled food. At last, the intense craving and the lunatic fright became so strong that he suddenly felt another rush of adrenaline, the same strange rush which he had felt as he finally awoke from his state of half-unconsciousness, during his first sleep here. The rush was foreign, but powerful, and Drake felt that he could conquer anybody and anything. He could even perhaps fight Noitan and the Enigami, if it meant that he was to have the bread and cheese. With adrenaline coursing through his veins, Drake dashed forward with such force that the deck rattled. He clawed ferociously at the Enigami, foam trickling down his neck and onto his shirt and spattering the deck. Noitan and the Enigami stood motionless, unmoved by the fit of aggression, and instead of dropping the plates of bread and cheese where Drake could reach them, they reached out their wrinkled, ashen hands, and flung Drake inside the building.

Drake got up, feeling nothing but the instinct to survive. He noticed the forbidden door to the upstairs and observed a steamy mist escaping the open entrance. He dashed toward it, believing that it was his only hope. Maybe his room was in there. But no! Drake stopped in his tracks. His room was brown! He couldn't go in there anymore. He didn't want anyone to hold his hand in the dark. But, still, it was less brown in there than it was out here. He rushed toward the door once more. He barely felt alive, and it was as though his brain was using every ounce of strength to simply stay within the bounds of reality and consciousness. His wrist hurt. Scratch. Pain. As he entered through the door, he heard a gigantic rushing sound, like a violent wind, and the ringing in his ears stopped. The sound was of the gigantic cloaks moving through the air as Noitan and the Enigami rushed after him. He quickened his pace and flung his arms forward as though this would make him reach the top of the stairs more swiftly. Foam continued to gush from his mouth as he rushed up the stairs in pursuit of urgent escape. His brain felt tight and compressed as Noitan and the Enigami seemed to gain on him. Ouch. His wrist hurt. His wrist was brown. Dull brown. Animalistic sounds escaped from his lips every few seconds as his feet pounded each stair. Grunting made him feel better and provided him with momentary relief from the present mental and physical trauma. Drake's ears rang with the sinister repetition of the Enigami: "Drink. Drink. Drink." The perpetual sound was like a siren blaring continuously, but in a whisper.

At last, he reached the top of the stairs and discovered a dark hall lay out before him. Despite the almost pitch-black atmosphere, and his crazed state, he noticed the impression of an ancient palace with pictures lining the walls and wooden tables lined with red velvet cloth. The red hue of the velvet seemed to stand out evilly, and Drake's mind was impressed with malice, as though in an unreal dream. He began to make his way ahead aggressively, rushing into the darkness, madly and blindly. As the blackness enveloped him, he could no longer make out any shapes, even faint ones. He could, quite literally, see nothing. It was only his sharp instinct that kept him from stumbling, injuring himself, and allowing the Enigami to come closer and overtake him. The ringing in his ears continued, and he covered them desperately, trying to shut out the fearful noise, but it was useless. It was as though the Enigami were present within his very brain.

"Drink. Drink. Drink."

The sound was part of him and had been encrypted into his mind. He could not rid himself of the thoughts.

"Drink. Drink. Drink."

They might soon control him. They might convince him to drink the liquid that would surely kill him. He might lose all control and.... Suddenly, Drake screamed, seized one of the tables with an unexpected strength and hurled it in the direction in which he knew the Enigami were coming.

He shrieked at the top of his lungs, "I do NOT want anyone to hold my hand in the dark!!"

Although, these words were less than comprehensible as he said them. He turned to his right and began to bang on the wall, madly, as though banging would increase his chances of being set free from his prison. BANG! BANG! BANG! BANG!

"Drink. Drink. Drink."

BANG! BANG! BANG! BANG!

"Drink. Drink. Drink."

Drake continued to pound the wall until, through his hazy cognition, he realized that the wall was a door. He grasped the knob. He felt himself spinning and shifting in the pure darkness. He turned the knob, but the door was locked. He began to tug the knob. He yanked until it fell off. He banged on the door yet again. BANG! BANG! BANG! BANG! He was barely conscious.

"Drink. Drink. Drink."

Suddenly, the adrenaline surged within him, once again, and he rammed two giant holes in the door with his fists. He continued to smack and smash the door until it came off its hinges and lay only halfway attached to the frame. Drake rushed into the room behind the door, as light streamed into the darkness from inside.

The room before him spun viciously, and Drake felt as though he were on an amusement park ride that would never stop. The room was simple and the furniture out of place, as though it were simply being stored within the room. It was full of dusty wooden cabinets and random cupboards. At one end, there were wooden tables holding strange bowls of unidentifiable powders and pastes. The most bizarre aspect of the room was that which did not belong. Drake's insides began to tremble as he saw that the center of the room was buried in the same bread and cheese that he craved. Without thought, he rushed to the pile, threw his face down into the mass of nutrients, and lapped them up, as a dog laps up water. He gorged on the enormous meal until his stomach felt sick. He continued to hear the ringing and covered his ears again as he ate, but this did nothing to stop the sound. Foam poured from his mouth in mad torrents. His cold blue eyes were now hot and veiny with aggression and fear. Drake mumbled as he continued to cram his mouth with the moldy morsels. His words were incoherent and jumbled in a strange hash of nonsense. When he had finished every crumb, he realized that the Enigami were coming and were next to the door. Panic seized him even more strongly than before. The fear almost paralyzed his limbs, but time was of the essence. He dashed frantically to the cabinet farthest from the door, one conveniently stored behind a larger cupboard, and concealed himself within its frame. He shook as he heard the Enigami enter the room. He ground his wrist into the wood within the cabinet, determined to get rid of the brown and paint the inside of his dark hiding place bright red. He clawed at his ears as the ringing became unbearable.

"DRINK. DRINK. DRINK."

Every second he passed within the cabinet, he felt that the Enigami would come find him and everything would be over. His biggest fear would become reality, and there would be nothing left.

"DRINK. DRINK. DRINK."

Drake reached for his ears again, but to his horror, he found that he was unable to move his arm. In a panic, Drake shook his leg, but it would not shake. He wanted to shout for help, but his vocal cords were also paralyzed. Nothing was functioning as it should, and Drake felt that this must be unreal, but nonetheless, the trepidation he felt was very real, indeed. Drake fainted.

Four
UMBER

Ringing ears. Pounding from outside on the cabinet. Paralysis. Can't move. NO!!! NO!!! Enigami. They'll come. They'll get you when you're paralyzed and make you

DRINK DRINK DRINK!!!!

Foam. Where is all this foam coming from?

DRINK DRINK DRINK!!!

Lonely is good! I don't want anyone to hold my hand in the dark!! My wrist hurts. I don't want to

DRINK DRINK DRINK!!!

Pounding. Paralysis. Foam. Where is all this foam coming from? Foam is water. Water is bad. Wa-wa-wa-ter.

DRINK DRINK DRINK!!!

Wa-wa-wa-ter. Adrenaline rush! No more paralysis. Pounding. Noitan? Pounding. Noitan is here! He will make me

DRINK DRINK DRINK!!!!

I don't want to drink foam. I don't want it. Foam is wa-wa-wa-ter. Wa-wa-wa-ter is bad. Clawing the air. Clawing the air helps with insanity. It makes you feel more alone, so they don't hold your hand in the dark. It makes the colors brighter and the sounds softer...

OUCH OUCH! My wrist hurts.

BANG! Break the cabinet! BANG!!! BANGBANGBANG-BANGBANG BREAK!!! Free! Enigami! No! Water glass. TERROR! KILL THE ENIGAMI!!! KILL THEM!!! NO!!!

Run! Run away and claw the air. It helps with insanity. It makes the colors brighter and the sounds softer. It takes away the brown.

The door! Kick it down!! Get OUT!! Get away from the brown foam! I don't want to...

DRINK DRINK DRINK!!!!

Stairs! Go down. Down is away from water. It's less brown down there. Where is all this foam coming from? Foam is water. Water is bad.

DRINK DRINK DRINK!!!

THEY'LL KILL ME!! BUT I'LL KILL THEM FIRST!!! No. Run. Do not kill. To kill makes the foam gush. Noitan is here. He is coming. Run! Do not kill. Do not kill. If you kill you will be brown. RUN! OUT THE DOOR! ALMOST AWAY.

DRINK DRINK DRINK!!!

NO!!! NO BROWN FOAM!!! WHERE IS ALL THIS FOAM COMING FROM!!!? WATER IS BAD!!! BAD!! BAD!! Outside. Sun. Hot. I hate heat. It hurts. I'm sick. Its more brown out here, but they're coming!

DRINK DRINK DRINK!!

THEY'RE COMING!! THEY'RE COMING WITH BROWN FOAM TO DRINK DRINK DRINK!!! NO!!!! NO!!!! I CAN'T!!! I CANNOT!!!

Clawing the air. Clawing will help. It will help. Colors brighter and sounds softer. It will help me be alone. Get rid of the brown. WA-WA-WA-TER!!! My wrist hurts. My wrist is brown. Cat and dog. They are here. They are not brown. Don't hold my hand in the dark, cat and dog. My wrist is brown. Leave me alone. I want to be alone because I am brown. They all hate me. I have no friends because I am brown. Where is all this foam coming from?

I can't breathe.

Cat and dog. They are not brown. They are talking. It hurts my ears. My ears hurt. My ears are brown.

I can't breathe.

JUMP! They said JUMP!!! JUUUUUUUMMMMMPPPP-PP!!!!!!

I...
CAN'T...
BREATHE!!

Silence. "Hold my hand...in...th-the dark." Consciousness...is.... gone. Drake is gone...

Drake is brown.

EPILOGUE

Journal Entry #79:

It has been a while since I have written. However, such an interesting occurrence of events must be recorded, so that the world will understand what is about to take place...that is...if the world still exists at a point when these events can be deemed history. My patient was male. His ID said that his name was "Drake", 22 years old, Caucasian, dark wavy hair...brown eyes. He was dead when we found him. He was lying on the road at the edge of an old, dilapidated building. His wrist was bleeding, caused by a large, festering bite wound. Some of his hair looked as though it had been torn out in clumps. Foam was pouring from his mouth in spurts, even though he was no longer alive. It was collecting in a very large pool around his head. I, and my other emergency physicians, had to be careful not to come into contact with the foam when removing the body, as foam pouring from the mouth is a classic symptom of rabies, and it is very contagious. We took the utmost care and collected a bit of the foam in a test tube. What we discovered when we brought it back to the lab was more than disturbing. Our patient apparently died of a strangely "futuristic" variant of the rabies virus...one that should not technically exist. The original virus kills the victim gradually after symptoms appear. However, once symptoms occur (usually two months after exposure), there is no treatment. This particular variant causes symptoms within a few hours, so that there is barely any time to seek treatment. To make matters worse, there is no current treatment for this variant at all.

My team and I explored the house. The first story was a dark-looking room with some stained glass windows, a small table, a battered crimson couch, a desk, and a lamp. We also found a door that, at first, appeared to be locked but was not. Behind it were some stairs, and we climbed to the second story. We found a room, at the beginning of a long hall, with a door that looked as though it had been torn viciously from its hinges. My team and I entered cautiously. The most shocking thing we found as we entered the room was a pile of numerous dead bodies, all wearing white lab coats and dressed in medical attire. They were each holding various medical instruments and had stains of a strange nature on each of their lab coats. They were all deformed and pallid. One of the bodies, in particular, stood out from the others. He had very pale skin, a short grey beard, and was wearing the clothing of a very prestigious doctor. His eyes were a very unearthly light grey. The entire room had a disheveled aura to it. There were random cabinets and medical equipment in every corner. One might describe it as a household lab. In the center of the room, we found a very large pile of strange substances. It is hard to describe these substances, only that they resembled...oh...say...moldy bread and cheese...in texture and appearance. We took a few of these with us, as samples, back to the lab. What we found in the lab was astonishing. We discovered that the strange substances were actually the failed attempts of an antidote for this unusual variant of rabies. However, the substances were so far away from an actual antidote that the best they could accomplish would probably be to slightly lessen symptoms as much as is already possible here at the hospital. However, with vigorous research and experimental work, the antidote might prove useful within the next 10 years. But will there be a world to save in 10 years' time? The rabies virus is now released into the world, and it is stronger than ever. We have never seen a variant so aggressive, so vigorous, so determined.

Perhaps the most terrifying thing of all, and I am hesitant to write it for fear that my own heart will realize that it is true: this variant becomes airborne after a certain period of time. Yes. The unthinkable has become reality.

Rabies is airborne.

My team and I are at a loss to understand how this could be possible, but our tests show that it is. It is in the AIR. The virus is spreading into the farthest corners of the world, even as I sit here writing. How did my team and I survive?

We were fortunate enough to find Drake before this virulent strain of the virus had become airborne. We were possibly witnesses to the very first moment of rabies becoming airborne. A few days after we had found Drake, subsequent lab tests showed the virus mutating to become airborne within the tube. There will be many deaths. As a doctor, this breaks my heart. There will be so many inevitable deaths. I can do nothing about it. However, my team and I, as well as other doctors in our area, are taking every precaution we possibly can. We have contacted the necessary people, and they will spread the information to the rest of the world. The quarantine has begun. But perhaps it is all in vain.

Of course, there is more to the story: the story of Nathan Cullah, the man we found dead among the numerous other bodies. He was the body that stood out among the others; the one with the unearthly grey eyes. When my team and I were exploring the house, a journal was found next to him, which is partially how we gleaned the information I am about to share with you. Nathan was a renowned scientist and doctor many years ago. One day, Nathan's son was bitten by a squirrel, and the child didn't tell him about it. After a few months, Nathan's son began to show the symptoms of rabies. Once a person shows the symptoms of rabies, nothing can be done for them. Nathan was horrified and heartbroken, and he rushed his son to the hospital where he worked. He cared for his son, himself, along with a team of loyal doctors, nurses, and technicians. Unfortunately, he had to endure the torture of watching his son go through bouts of insanity, unspeakable pain, and a fear of drinking the most basic substance: water. Finally, Nathan's son died in the hospital. Nathan was a changed man, but not the kind of change one hopes for in a man. Grief did him in. He vowed to cure the rabies virus once and for all, which would appear to be a noble cause, until one learns how he went about it. Nathan left his job and took a team of loyal doctors, nurses, and medical specialists, who were also secretly interested in medical experimentation, along with him.

Nathan lived in the building, near the area where we found Drake, working on his rabies cure. His lab was in the room where we found the strange "moldy bread and cheese" substances. The medical specialists would visit him every day to work on the antidote. Nathan was obsessed, and he would not eat, sleep, or drink for days. Nathan's companions noticed his lack of self-care and pointed it out to him, but he brushed it off, coldly. Brainwashed by Nathan, and believing in the cause, they ignored his strange behavior and carried on to find a cure. Eventually, tiredness and lack of nourishment led to a lack of judgment, and Nathan injected himself with the original rabies virus. He madly reasoned that this would motivate him to find the antidote. If he couldn't save himself, he couldn't save anyone. He told his staff not to visit anymore. He was going to finish this alone. The days passed, and Nathan could find no cure. Eventually, the symptoms of rabies set in, and Nathan found himself becoming less and less able to reason. His mind was slowly going. Within day 3 of his symptoms, he had, while attempting to create an antidote, inadvertently created a more powerful variant of rabies (the variant we now deal with, inevitably). This variant was stronger, more aggressive, survived longer, ...and could become airborne, as we see now.

The others, worrying about Nathan, decided to visit again. Unfortunately, Nathan had brainwashed them to such a point that he convinced them all to be injected with the virus, telling them that they had to be motivated to find the cure. Nathan injected them all with the newer and more potent version of the virus. They lost their cognitive abilities sooner than Nathan had, and they decided to worship him as a god because he had infected them with his new virus. As they decided this, they heard the sounds of a stray cat and dog wandering around outside the building. They rushed outside, grabbed the animals, and injected them with the strain as a sacrifice to their new god. Nathan was the first leader of a rabies cult...and it was a deadly one.

All of this information we deduced from the fragmented thoughts written in his journal, as well as obvious signs and other artifacts about the building. We can only conclude that this is about the time Drake came along and was infected by the first strain. The virus was still in its early stages and had not become airborne yet, so the newer variant was transmitted to Drake through a bite. He was infected in the normal way, but endured the horror of a virus more powerful than any ever seen before. It is quite possible that the cult made some kind of contact around that time, as we know that Drake went into the building (we found some of his DNA on a half-drunk water glass on a table, inside). Perhaps he had to endure the awful presence of Nathan and his cult while he suffered.

So, there it is. There is the horrific situation of the current world and the haunting tale of Nathan Cullah. One man's intense love for his son would cause the death of the world. Was he a hero because he loved? Or was he a villain because he killed? Drake was one of Nathan's first victims, and there will absolutely be many more. If only Nathan could have understood what he created. He has perhaps caused the end of the world. Who knew that love would be the cause for the end of the world.

But now...I must...I must...go. For I do not...feel...feel quite well at all. My head aches...I...I am very thirsty. The world is now under quarantine, but the virus is in the air, and all we can do is claw at the air. It makes the colors brighter and the sounds softer. Where...where is all this foam coming from? The virus is rushing in the currents of the wind. And it waits...brownly.

THE WORLD UNDONE

Oh, Nathan! He, a man, who loved via hate,
  A hatred for the virus, which caused Drake's fate;
But the world is now in peril, and it's Noitan's fault,
Nothing can be done to stop the virus's assault.
It rushes in the wind, and carries with the mist,
The world is slowly dying,
Its brain is liquifying,
And I would be lying,
if I didn't tell you this:
Rabies.
The futuristic variant is free,
Nothing can be done, and you cannot flee.

Acknowledgements

I am very thankful to those who assisted me in this magical journey of bringing Drake and the dull brown room to life.

To my beta readers, who trusted me with their minds, and were the first to meet Drake. Thank you, Madeline Bedrosian, David Boyer, Avrey Coble, Cindy Jenkins, Gary Jenkins, Casey King, Dr. Andrea Leonard, Paul Mullins, Kinsleigh Powell, and Kerry Williams.

To my ARC readers, who helped me build support for *Rabid*. There were so many of you. Thank you all very much.

To my supportive family, who always cheer me on in everything I do. Thank you to my parents: Phil and Holly Powell. Thank you to my siblings: Chase, Josiah, Kinsleigh, and Reese Powell.

To my amazing editors, Wendy Claunch and Dr. Andrea Leonard. Thank you for being mentors to me and guiding me in this process.

Thank you to everyone who supported me and helped me believe in this story.

AUTHOR'S NOTE

When I first told people I was writing a book, they would often say, "I didn't know you wrote." To which my reply was almost always, "I didn't know, either." Of course, this was not entirely true. I had written books of poems ever since I was a teenager. However, I had never tried to publish an entire story before. So, here we are.

The inspiration for the story came, interestingly enough, from two dreams that I had before I began writing *Rabid*. The first dream is hard for me to remember. I do, however, seem to remember it having something to do with a rabid animal. I seem to remember that, when I awoke the next morning, I was so intrigued, that I began vigorously researching rabies and its symptoms. The common knowledge on the subject indicated that rabies was always fatal when symptoms showed. There was no hope when someone began to feel the effects of this virus. It affected the brain, which made it very psychological. How interesting.

The second dream, that inspired *Rabid*, was very strange, indeed. I remember standing on top of a building, and then suddenly looking down and realizing that the building was much higher than I had first thought it was. Perhaps it had moved upward. It was so strange and intriguing that I remember thinking, "I need to write a book about this". This dream was actually the inspiration for Drake's very first hallucination in the first chapter.

Ah, yes. And now we come to the question of Drake. Drake; an intelligent mind, a serious demeanor, and yet a deeply feeling soul. Who is he? Where did he come from? Is he a real person? Well...yes. Drake is a self-insert. Drake is me. Yes. I deliberately gave him my icy blue eyes, curly dark brown hair, and serious personality. I relate to Drake on a very personal level, and a lot of the way he thinks is the way that I think, as well.

An interesting thing about Drake is the fact that he is very serious, and almost cold, on the outside. However, he is very warm, empathetic, and emotional inside. He is a beautifully crafted epitome of the phrase "still waters run deep". The fact that Drake feels so deeply makes the predicament of his humanity and loneliness all the more heart-wrenching. He is sorely misunderstood; however, the deep understanding of Drake's complex mind, which is attained through reading *Rabid,* hopefully, makes the reader want to befriend him, to be on his side.

Now that I release Drake, his complex and very human self, into the world, he will never be lonely again. He will live on, and his favorite dark room, with his circles of friends, will never be brown. Dull brown.

ABOUT THE AUTHOR

 Andalyn Powell currently resides in Roanoke, Virginia. She earned her IT degree from Liberty University. In her spare time, she is a weightlifting enthusiast whose favorite lift is bench press. She is also an actor in her home community theatre at Attic Productions in Fincastle, Virginia, where she enjoys fully immersing herself in her characters and exploring their backstories.

She has always loved the concept of psychological horror and is excited to explore this genre through her debut book *Rabid*. Andalyn's favorite thing about her book is her very personal character, Drake. Andalyn hopes that readers will love, understand, and perhaps even resonate with Drake as much as she does.

♪ tiktok.com/@andalyn.powell.au

◉ instagram.com/andalynpowell_author

f facebook.com/share/1UD8mq94sM/

LEAVE A REVIEW

Did you enjoy reading *Rabid*?

If the dull brown room has left a lasting impression on you...

If Drake resonated with you in some way...

If you found yourself both intrigued and entertained...

Would you consider leaving a review to support this story?

Help keep the insanity alive by leaving a review of the book on Amazon.com.

Inside the Mind of Rabid

Do you ever wonder what is behind the insanity? What is going on inside the mind of *Rabid*?

The Inside the Mind of *Rabid* newsletter shares chilling stories about how the world of the dull brown room was conceived.

If original story outlines, author stories, and sneak peeks at new books make your mind tingle in anticipation, subscribe using the link below!

https://substack.com/@andalynpowell

www.ingramcontent.com/pod-product-compliance
Lightning Source LLC
LaVergne TN
LVHW020419070526
838199LV00055B/3668